COMBING THROUGH TANGLETOWN

Written by

Ron Philippe

To my father,

When we meet again we'll read this book together just like the old times.

But for now, rest peacefully old soldier.

CHAPTER ONE

"**8**, 9, 10, more months until we're back in NewComb for summer and I can't wait!" Braidy Stylez told her twin brother, Wavey.

"Can you stop counting already? It's making my head hurt," Wavey replied.

The two sat next to each other on a crowded bus filled with students ready for their first day of school.

"I'm going to countdown every day until we're outta this place," Braidy responded.

"It's only our first day here and you're already complaining. You don't even know how it's going to be," Wavey answered optimistically.

Braidy stood up and looked around the whole bus. As she sat down, her facial expression changed.

"What's wrong? Is everything alright?" Wavey asked, sensing that something was wrong with his sister.

"I'm fine, I just miss NewComb, that's all," she answered.

"Okay, but no matter what, I always have your back, Braidy. Remember that." Wavey assured his sister who was visibly bothered.

The bus made its way to the entrance of the school. A large sign at the top of the main entrance read, **TANGLETOWN JR. HIGH SCHOOL**.

Under the sign, stood a tall man with an evil look on his face, eyeballing all of the students that were entering the school building. Both Wavey and Braidy heard students on the bus whispering, "Mr. Licer is here." Every one of them contained a sense of worry in their voice.

"C'mon, let's go, Braidy," Wavey said, as the students exited the bus.

Braidy decided to remain in her seat until they were the last ones left before exiting.

"Let's go before I drag you off this bus by your braids," Wavey joked.

Braidy shot her brother an angry look and the two made their way towards the building with very different feelings towards their new school. Wavey smiled from ear to ear, excited about his first day there. On the contrary, Braidy was the complete opposite. She walked to her class, feeling lost and uncomfortable. As they approached the building, Mr. Licer shot them an evil look.

While most kids are excited to move and make new friends, the Stylez twins not so much. After Mr. Stylez received a new job opportunity, the Stylez family moved to Tangletown, Hairisota from NewComb City, which was a completely different environment from what the Stylez twins were used to. The move hit Braidy the hardest. She left behind her friends, her school, and her sense of comfortability. She was able to be herself there. Now she was afraid of this transition to her new school.

As Braidy and her brother walked to their classrooms, she paid close attention to her surroundings, especially the students, who appeared to be nothing like their old friends in NewComb. They knew it would take a lot of getting used to for Braidy, as she was not a fan of such drastic changes.

"Room 55- Ms. Frobe," Braidy read the sign attached next to the large classroom door.

"What kind of name is Frobe," Wavey joked.

"Oh, shut up and don't embarrass us like you always do Wavey," Braidy said, as she opened the classroom door. She opened the door slowly, causing it to make a long screeching noise which drew the attention of everyone in the classroom.

Shocked and nervous, Braidy and Wavey stood in the front of the class silent.

"You two must be the Stylez twins," a loud voice said as she laid eyes on the twins. Their eyes widened as if they saw a ghost.

"Y- yes we are," said Braidy to the lady standing before them.

"I'm Ms. Frobe. Welcome to 6th grade here at Tangletown Jr. High. You guys can have a seat right here."

Ms. Frobe placed them in the middle of the classroom. As they walked to their seats, Braidy felt the eyes of the students staring at them.

"Do you see this lady's hair?" Wavey whispered to his sister, referring to Ms. Frobe.

Ms. Frobe stood in the front of the classroom, a tall skinny lady wearing a white button down shirt with a little peace sign pin on the front, an afro as big as the sun and a smile just as bright. She introduced herself to the class and told the students a little bit about herself.

My name is Ms. Frobe and I have been teaching here for 30 years, but I am originally from NewComb City." As soon as the twins heard that, their faces lit up.

"So far, I like Frobe. She seems cool," Braidy said with a smile.

Ms. Frobe opened the class with an icebreaker. "In order for me to get to know you all a little better, I would like for each of us to say your name and a fun fact. I'll go first, my name is Ms. Frobe, and I haven't cut my hair in over 40 years." The students were shocked and amazed, some even asked to touch it. Each student had a chance to share and eventually it was Wavey's turn.

"My name is Wavey Stylez, and I got the best waves at Tangletown Jr. high."

The class became silent, not understanding what he was talking about.

"Ya'll don't see these spinners?!" Wavey added enthusiastically, while rubbing his head. A bunch of 'Oooo's' and 'Ahhh's' followed directly after. The students lowered their voices and Braidy shared a few words.

"My name is Braidy Stylez and I... I..." Braidy instantly became nervous and decided not to share anymore. In the back of the room, two students were laughing hysterically, which made Braidy feel more uncomfortable.

"Hey, cut it out!" Ms. Frobe called out.

"Who are those guys laughing at me like that?" Braidy asked the student next to her.

"Those boys? Oh, that's Buzz and Fade, the Frizz twins. They're such bullies and they think that they run Tangletown Jr. High," the girl replied.

Braidy looked at them and noticed the two boys; both with terrible haircuts, and clothes that barely fit. The class continued to share and there was one more student left to go. He got up from his seat and was very small for a 6th grader. As he started to speak, he appeared to be very timid.

"My name is Patrick Growth and I - "
Before he had a chance to finish, he was
rudely interrupted.

"And you're short and ugly with all of
those bald spots in your head."

Patrick took a seat and put his head
down while the class and the Frizz twins
laughed at him.

"That's it, Buzz and Fade step
outside, we need to talk!" Ms. Frobe
ordered them.

Braidy noticed Patrick from her seat
and asked about him. "Who is that?"
Braidy asked her new found friend.

"I can't lie, he looks a little weird,"
Wavey added.

"Ohh, that's Patrick. No one knows
much about him because he stays to

himself all the time," the student told Braidy.

"So, what's up with his hair, why does it look like that?"

She continued. "No one knows. Some people think he has some type of disease, so they just stay away from him," the student replied.

"Diseassee?!" Wavey yelled.

"Can you keep it down, Wavey! Neither you, I, or anyone in the class knows what's wrong with him for that matter, so be quiet," Braidy scolded her brother.

Ms. Frobe and the Frizz twins came back into the classroom and as they walked back to their seats, they made hand gestures, making fun of Braidy's hair. She looked at them with a straight face, took a deep breath and in her mind and sarcastically thought, "Tangletown is gonna be a blast."

CHAPTER TWO

As days went by, Wavey tried to assure his sister that things will get better at Tangletown. "You just have to understand, Braidy. It's going to take some getting used to." Wavey said to Braidy, as he tied one of his many durags on his head.

"You just don't get it, I don't feel the same way I felt back at NewComb," Braidy replied, as she re-braided her hair.

"And why is that?" Wavey asked.

"WE BEEN THERE FOR FIVE DAYS ALREADY AND YOU HAVEN'T NOTICED?" Braidy yelled.

"Hey, hey, relax. What are you talking about?" Wavey was confused by his sister's outburst. Braidy took a deep breath, visibly annoyed.

"Nobody in Tangletown has hair like us, especially me! Nobody has braids, nobody even has waves like you! And if anything is different about your hair, we get treated differently. Kinda like that Patrick Growth kid," Braidy let out, loudly.

"Patrick Growth? You mean that weird kid that sits in the back of the class?" Wavey asked.

"He may look weird but, I think there's something going on with him. Leave him alone!" Braidy shouted.

"Alright, alright, fine. I mean, I didn't look at it like that, but I see what you're saying. So, what do you plan on doing? We can't just leave," Wavey explained.

Braidy took a deep sigh, "I don't know, Wavey but I hope it gets better eventually." Braidy finished braiding the rest of her hair before going to bed.

The next morning, the two woke up and got ready for school. "C'mon hurry up, you're going to make us late!" Braidy screamed while waiting at the door. Wavey ran down the steps, rushing at his sister's call. "You're gonna leave that on?" Braidy asked, referring to Wavey's durag.

"I bet you want to wear it," Wavey replied jokingly.

"HA! You wish. Now let's catch the bus before we miss it," Braidy said as they exited the house. They got on the bus and ended up sitting in front of the Frizz twins who were joking around and being disruptive.

"Ooo look, it's the Stylez twins. I'm Braidy, and I'm Wavey." They both chanted, making mocking gestures of Braidy and Wavey's hairstyles.

"Just ignore it, they're trying to get under your skin that's all," Wavey explained to his sister. Braidy became very frustrated and annoyed as she tried her best to stay calm. However, the Frizz twins continued with their jokes, only adding fuel to her temper.

What was supposed to be a 20-minute bus ride, felt like forever. "I thought you were always gonna have my back," Braidy said to her brother.

"What did you want me to do? Beat them up on the bus?" he replied.

"No, but you could have said something. They were being jerks to the both of us – and mom and dad always told us to stand up for ourselves," Braidy finished, still frustrated.

"It isn't that serious, they're just some bullies who are trying to get the best of us." Wavey shrugged.

The two argued as they walked towards the school, drawing attention from everyone, including Mr. Licer. "HEY, KEEP IT DOWN!" he shouted. Braidy and Wavey immediately stopped. Braidy looked up and saw this tall man with a blue suit, white shirt, and a bright red tie with little lice crawling all over him. They both got scared and walked away quickly.

"That Licer guy is creepy," Braidy said.

"Yeah, did you see all that lice on him? I'm staying away from that guy," replied Wavey. They got to their classroom and found the Frizz twins sitting in the seats that they originally claimed since the first day of school.

"Hey, those are our seats!" Braidy said as she approached the twins.

"Yeah, we've been sitting here since school started and you guys know that." Wavey chimed in.

The Frizz twins looked around and called out, "Hey, does anyone see Braidy or Wavey's name on these chairs because I don't. This is 6th grade now, there are no assigned seats like the ones in your baby school," Buzz shouted. Both the Stylez and the Frizz twins started to argue.

"HEY, THAT'S ENOUGH! Everyone find a seat and make it theirs!" Ms. Frobe intervened as she stopped writing on the board to tend to their situation.

"So, where are we gonna sit?" Wavey asked.

As they looked around, they noticed there were no empty seats besides the ones in the back of the room. The class points to the two seats in the back next to Patrick Growth.

"I don't wanna sit next to him, he's weird," whispered Wavey.

The two made their way to the empty seats, attempting to stay away from Patrick and the rest of the class. "I don't think I'm ever gonna like it here," Braidy said as she got ready for another long day of school at Tangletown Jr. high.

CHAPTER THREE

Feeling alone, the Stylez twins were the last ones left in the classroom as the other students departed for lunch. Ms. Frobe was grading assignments when she noticed them sitting by themselves with their heads down. "You guys aren't hungry today?" She asked.

"BLAME BRAIDY," Wavey said upset. "I wanted to go but she was like 'nooo let's wait here, I don't wanna go to lunch with those kids.' So, that's why we're still sitting here." Braidy rolled her eyes as her brother mimicked her.

"Well, why not?" Ms. Frobe pressed. "I know you guys are new, but Tangletown may take some getting used to and you'll make friends in no time," she finished with a warm smile.

"Well, it sure doesn't feel like it," Braidy added.

Ms. Frobe pulled up a chair and sat closer to them. "What does it feel like then? I think I may have an idea." She asked, concerned.

"I don't wanna talk about it." Braidy said lowly.

"I've been working here for a very long time, and I also come from NewComb City just like you." Ms. Frobe started, "If you ever want to talk or need help with anything, my door is always open, especially for fellow NewCombers." Ms. Frobe assured the twins.

"C'mon Braidy, tell her what you told me," Wavey pushed.

"I said NO, Alright!" She exclaimed. Braidy then got up from her seat and proceeded to walk out of the classroom.

"Where are you going?" Wavey asked.

"To Lunch!" Braidy replied.

Wavey rushed after his sister, and as they walked through the halls, Braidy saw some of the students looking at her and whispering amongst themselves.

"She's so angry, and her hair looks crazy. No wonder why she sat in the back with Patrick, they've both got crazy hair." She caught a few of the mean comments as she walked past a group of kids. As they made their way to the cafeteria, they were suddenly stopped.

"Excuse me," a loud voice yelled out. Braidy and Wavey stared at the man towering over them, in fear. "Stylez twins, huh? The man says chuckling. As he spoke, Wavey noticed Buzz and Frizz as they watched the scene from a distance. "My name is Mr. Licer and if you didn't know I am the principal here at Tangletown Jr. High." Still scared and confused, Braidy and Wavey just stood there, shocked that the principal was speaking to them. He continued, "We have rules and regulations which need to be followed here at Tangletown Jr. High and unfortunately, YOU are not following them." Mr. Licer exclaimed as he pointed to Braidy.

Braidy instantly became defensive and shouted, "How!?" Confused at Mr. Licer's confrontation.

"Your hairstyle is just not appropriate for this school." Mr. Licer spit out.

Angrily, Braidy asked, "Well what's not "appropriate" about it? People in Tangletown have all types of hairstyles, just look around." As they looked around the hallway, they noticed the other girls with curls, straight hair, pony tails, and other styles. But nobody had long braids like Braidy.

"Listen, rules are rules, and this isn't up for discussion. It's either you cut it, change it, cover it up, or do something about it because this is not acceptable."

Braidy's face displayed instant defeat. "But I just-," she tried to explain herself.

"I just said this isn't up for discussion!" Mr. Licer shouted, while pulling out detention slips.

"But, I didn't know," she quickly let out.

"I tried to warn you, but since you two wanna argue, how about you do that at detention." Mr. Licer scolded and wrote their names down on the slip. Braidy rolled her eyes while she waited for Mr. Licer to finish writing their detention slips. They took the slips from Mr. Licer and walked away angrily. *What a horrible first experience with their new school principal*, they both thought.

Braidy and Wavey finally retrieved their lunches and sat at an empty table in the corner of the cafeteria. "Okay, so now I really hate it here," Braidy said as she threw the lunch on the table. "And I really don't like Mr. Licer," she threw in.

"You didn't need to try and go back and forth with him," Wavey added, as he started to eat lunch. "We are new here and it's just gonna take some getting used to, but we're gonna be good," he assured his sister. Keeping a calm but bothered demeanor

As Braidy ate her lunch, she noticed the Frizz twins watching them from a distance as they laughed and whispered to each other. Buzz looked at Braidy and made gestures mocking her braids. She turned and looked away, deciding not to give them any type of attention. "I also don't like those Frizz twins. They think they're slick, making fun of other people's hair and stuff."

The school day came to an end, but unfortunately not for Braidy and Wavey. "Detention in the first month of school, great," Wavey said sarcastically. As they arrived at the detention room, they realized that Ms. Frobe will be the teacher supervising them. Braidy was immediately relieved as the stress of detention went away.

"I'm surprised to see you two in here," says Ms. Frobe.

"BLAME BRAIDY," Wavey sighed and pointed to his sister.

The two went back and forth until Ms. Frobe broke up their argument. "Alright, that's enough. One of you tell me what happened." The twins look at each other for a moment and Braidy started to speak.

"So, after we left your classroom, we were walking to the cafeteria right and Mr. Licer, with his big ole ugly lice having-self told me that I had to cut my hair or cover it up. Can you believe that!" Braidy blurted out. Ms. Frobe laughed and shook her head at Braidy's dramatized version of the story.

"What happened?" Wavey asked Ms. Frobe.

"I am not surprised at all. Tangletown has changed a lot over the years and now people want to make it look a certain way. We used to be a school that embraced everyone's differences and welcomed them with open arms as long as they were willing to be hard working students. Their hair didn't matter. Your hair is what makes you YOU. It's what puts a smile on your face in the morning and makes you feel comfortable. I cannot tell you what to do but, what I can tell you is think about what Mr. Licer said and try to think outside the box. Maybe you might find a way to get around his rules." Wavey and Braidy sat there and thought about everything Ms. Frobe said.

"So should we... I don't know Ms. Frobe interjects or what about... hey I don't know Ms. Frobe says again. Think smarter not harder," Ms. Frobe tells them, as the bell concluding detention rings. Wavey and Braidy stood there and thought further. After a while, Wavey's mind began to wander. Although he was still upset about detention his face lit up with ideas.

CHAPTER FOUR

After a long and stressful day, Braidy and Wavey made their way home on the school bus. A feeling of disappointment after Mr. Licer's cruel treatment of them still lingered in their minds. "I just don't get it. Like he didn't have to give us detention" Braidy said breaking their silence.

"Maybe if you've kept your mouth shut and didn't try and have an argument WITH THE PRINCIPAL OF THE SCHOOL, we wouldn't be in this position," Wavey sneered.

"So, what did you want me to do? Just stay quietly while he treated me unfairly? He only pointed at me Wavey, meanwhile everyone else in Tangletown is able to embrace their own hairstyles. Why can't I?" Braidy asked, saddened by her replay of the day's events.

"Listen Braidy, I don't know but, wait till mom and dad find out about how YOU got us into detention." Wavey could not get over the consequences of Braidy's debate.

"Whatever Wave, you never wanna be on my side."

As they made their way inside the house, Wavey slammed the door behind him, which let off a loud echo throughout the entire house.

Mr. Stylez approached the kids and asked, "What's the matter?"

Wavey didn't hesitate before answering, "BLAME BRAIDY!" He screamed as he and his sister stomped up the stairs. Mr. and Mrs. Stylez decided to follow them up to their rooms to see what was going on. Mr. Stylez checked on Braidy while Mrs. Stylez checked on Wavey. Mr. Stylez knocked on the door gently and heard his daughter cry while he waited for her to answer. "Braidy? It's daddy. Can I come in?" He asked gently, as he cracked open the door.

"No!" she screamed.

"Well, I hear you crying, and I need to know why." Mr. Stylez said as he slowly opened the door wider. Braidy sat on the edge of her bed, slouched over, and crying into her arms. Mr. Stylez came and sat next to her, rubbing her back to console her. "Let's talk about it, it's alright," he said as he hugged her shoulders tight.

Braidy took a deep breath and let it all out, "It's Tangletown alright! It's coming to this stupid place for no reason. Everything was fine back home, and we just had to move. We left my friends and my school just to come to this horrible place and I hate it!" Braidy shouted so loud that she was heard all the way from across the hall in Wavey's room where he and Mrs. Stylez were. As they heard Braidy vent, they got up to walk to Braidy's room to hear more of what she was saying. "And then today, the principal out of nowhere singles me out and said that my hairstyle is inappropriate for this school and-."

Mrs. Stylez jumped in and shouted, "HE SAID WHAT!?" Mrs. Stylez's anger grew within seconds.

"Yes, mom. He said the braids in my hair were inappropriate and that I had to cut it, change it or cover it up." Braidy tells her mother exactly what Mr. Licer told her.

"What about your brother? Where was he?" Mrs. Stylez asked, trying to calm down.

"He was right there, and he didn't even have my back, he never does. It's like he never thinks about how things make me feel. He's only upset that I made us get detention earlier today, but it's still unfair."

Wavey stood behind the door as Braidy spoke to their parents. A feeling of regret and sadness instantly came over him. *Maybe I'm not a good brother*, he thought. His mood changed from anger to sadness as he headed back to his room without anyone noticing.

Wavey laid on his bed and the ideas he had thought of earlier during detention start going through his mind.

As he looked around this room, he noticed his wall of durags. He grabbed the only bright pink one that he owned and looked at it. Would it work? Could it work? Would Braidy like it? I mean she said she wouldn't wear it, so why bother? But hmm, maybe if she wore it in a different way, she might like it. Maybe if I give her my pink one because she likes pink? But why would she wear it, she doesn't like wearing anything on her head because she loves showing off her hair. All of these thoughts ran through Wavey's mind. "UGHHHHHH," he let out. He threw the durag onto the floor in frustration and hopped on the bed, stuffing his face in the pillow. Slowly, the sound of his sister's voice began to fade away as he heard a knock on his bedroom door.

"Come in," he called out, trying to get himself together. Mrs. Stylez walked into the room.

"It's so messy in here," she said after tripping over the durag.

"Hey, be careful mom, that's for Braidy," Wavey said as he picked it up.

"I thought this was your durag. Why are you giving it to your sister and why is it on the floor?" Mrs. Stylez asked while dusting it off.

"Because I'm a bad brother and I want to make things right," Wavey replied.

"Well, there's no need to do that. Your father and I are going up to that school first thing tomorrow morning to have a word with Mr. Licer," Mrs. Stylez answered sternly.

"NO! WAIT! Let me fix this," Wavey exclaimed.

Mrs. Stylez paused for a minute and then asked, "How are you going to fix this?"

Wavey instantly held up the durag and smiled. "With this, mom. Just trust me. We just started middle school, we don't need our parents coming in and embarrassing us," Wavey answered honestly.

Mrs. Stylez laughed, "We won't embarrass you. As your parents, we're here to defend you guys." Wavey felt a sense of comfortability with his mother's words, but insisted.

"Mom, please just trust me. I want to handle this," Wavey returned confidently. Mrs. Stylez stopped and thought briefly.

"Hmm alright. I'll go tell your father but, if this little plan of yours doesn't work, we're going to go up there to handle this ourselves." Mrs. Stylez suggested.

"Alright, understood!" Wavey quickly agreed.

As Mrs. Stylez left his room, Wavey closed the door behind her. He picked up the durag and walked to his mirror, trying to tie it in various ways that he thought Braidy might like. While doing so, he heard a knock on the door again. Thinking it was his mother, Wavey automatically answered, "Come in." Braidy slowly opened the door and immediately started to laugh.

"HAHAHA! Why are you wearing it like that?" She asked, referring to the durag on his head.

Wavey was shocked when he heard his sister's voice and quickly snatched off the durag. He turned around and asked, "Hey what are you doing in here? Shouldn't you be crying like a little baby."

Braidy, finished laughing, looked at her brother and said, "No, I actually came to say sorry. Sorry for being bratty, and getting us in trouble. I didn't mean for us to get detention."

Wavey looked at his sister surprised by her apology. "I actually wanted to say sorry to you. For not having your back as much as I should have, and not taking your side. I don't want to be a bad brother to you," Wavey answered disappointedly as he thought back to what happened hours earlier.

"You're a great brother, Wavey. I don't want you to think that, and I love you bro." Braidy extended her arms out to give her brother a hug. "Now, I just have one question."

"What's up?"

"What on earth were you doing with that?" Braidy laughed, pointing to the durag.

Wavey joined in the laugh and replied, "I actually wanted to give it to you. You know cause Mr. Licer did give you an option to cover it up."

Braidy looked at it and tried it on. "Hmm, isn't this for boys though?" She asked after she put on the durag.

"Not really, you can wear it too." Wavey replied.

"What if I wear it like this?" She asked after tying it one way.

"Eh."

Braidy then tried it on another way. "How about this?" Wavey stood observing Braidy's look.

"This is alright but, I think you can do better."

Braidy turned back to the mirror and tried a few more styles before turning around. "Okay what about this, Wavey?" She asked for the third time.

"PERFECT!" I think it looks great on you!" He exclaimed. Braidy tied the durag with a bow on the side of her head which hung down above her eye.

"You know what, I actually do look cute in this," Braidy said while looking at herself in the mirror.

"I'm still the cuter twin," Wavey joked. He grabbed his gold silky durag off the wall and put it on.

The twins ended up joking, laughing, and making funny faces in front of the mirror for their enjoyment. After a few hours of fooling around, the two end up separating. Braidy went to her room and Wavey stayed in his. Before leaving, Wavey told his sister, "I wonder if Mr. Licer is gonna say anything about this," referring to Braidy's new cover up.

"He shouldn't. He said cover it up and that's what I'm doing. Besides, I look cute in it anyway," she added jokingly.

"You're right," Wavey said happy he was able to turn Braidy's mood around. The two went to sleep hopeful about going to school the next day with their new looks together.

CHAPTER FIVE

After a series of hectic events the day before, the Stylez twins woke up and hoped that today would be better. Wavey ate breakfast and was ready for school, while his sister dragged her feet to put herself together.

"What are you waiting for?" Wavey shouted up the stairs.

"I want to find a cute outfit to match my new durag," Braidy shouted back, as she flipped her whole room around looking for something to wear.

After what seemed like an eternity, Braidy finally came downstairs wearing a brand-new outfit. She had on white sneakers, blue jeans, and a pink shirt to match her pink durag.

"I think that looks great," Wavey said, excited for Braidy's new found look.

"Now come on, let's catch the bus." Before leaving the house, Braidy noticed something. "Where is yours?" Braidy asked, pointing to Wavey's head.

"What?" he asked.

"Your durag, aren't you supposed to wear one?" Wavey shrugged his shoulders.

"Nah, I normally wear it to bed and leave it home before school to show off the spinners. You know that Braidy."

"Well yeah, but I thought we were gonna both wear them together. You know, like brother and sister," Braidy replied. Wavey thought about it briefly.

"Okay fine," he agreed. Wavey ran up to his room and opened his drawer of durags. "Which color?" He yelled out to his sister.

"Uhmmm green? You know pink and green are my favorite colors," Braidy shouted back.

"I was thinking gold," Wavey replied.

"Well just grab one of them quickly or we are going to miss the bus." Braidy answered frantically.

Wavey, stuck between the two, grabbed both colors and ran down the stairs and out the house. As the two walked to the bus stop, Wavey began tying the gold one. "Green would have looked better," Braidy added.

"Well I brought it with me in my bag. Maybe I'll wear it tomorrow." He replied after a moment.

"Orrr maybe I might wear it tomorrow," Braidy joked.

"Yeah we'll see about that." The two laughed it off and arrived at the bus stop. As the bus rolled in, they felt the eyes of the students looking at them through the window. They got on the bus and those same eyes continued to stare at them, as they heard students whispering under their breaths.

"What is that? Why are they wearing that? Where did they get those from?" The Tangletown students asked each other silently. The Stylez twins walked to the back of the bus where they found two empty seats and sat down. Across from them sat Patrick Growth, who sat by himself, with his head down, quietly waiting to arrive at school.

The bus made a stop to pick up a few students and the Frizz twins got on. They decided to sit behind Braidy and Wavey at the back of the bus.

"Nice scarves," Buzz says sarcastically.

"Looks more like a cheap hoodie," Frizz added.

As Buzz and Fade laughed with each other, Wavey noticed his sister getting visibly upset, but before she could say anything, he told her, "Just ignore them. You know they always try to get under our skin."

Braidy listened and calmed down and paid them no attention as they continued trying to make jokes. The twins eventually realized that the jokes were not affecting them, and noticed Patrick sitting by himself and started to pick on him.

"Hey Patrick, I think you need to be wearing one of those head rags to cover up all those spots." The Frizz twins yelled on the bus to Patrick which made everyone laugh. An upset Patrick didn't reply and put his face down in embarrassment, while all the students on the bus laughed at him.

"IT'S NOT FUNNY!" Braidy screamed in anger while everyone on the bus became silent. She looked over at Patrick who sat alone in the seat across from them and called him over. "Hey, Patrick, come here," she called.

Buzz noticed and replied, "Yeah, go to your little girlfriend."

Braidy sighed with annoyance and responded, "Be quiet, Buzz. Maybe you need to be wearing a durag yourself because that "Buzz" cut of yours is not it." Braidy blurted out.

"OOOOOOOOOOOOO," the students on the bus all ooed, which ultimately put pressure on Buzz. Both Buzz and Braidy stared at each other.

After a few moments, Wavey stood up and shouted, "Hey Mind your business Buzz!"

Fade tapped his brother's shoulder and whispered, "Just have a seat, it isn't worth it." Buzz sat down huffing and puffing. Patrick moved to the seat closest to Braidy and Wavey and talked with them for the remainder of the ride to school.

"Soooo, what's the situation with your hair? Are you going bald or is it just a bad haircut or something?" Wavey asked Patrick, waiting for a response.

"Ughh, don't pay my brother any mind. Sometimes he gets carried away and asks the wrong things," Braidy said while rolling her eyes.

"It's alright, I don't mind sharing. Besides, you guys are the only ones who spoke to me here, so it's good to have people to talk to." Patrick replied. "To answer your question though Wavey, I have a condition." Patrick answered.

"A condition?" The Stylez twins asked in unison.

"What do you mean? Like you're sick or something"? Braidy added, confused.

"No, no, no. I'm not sick or anything. I have a condition called alopecia-areata." The Stylez twins looked at each other for a second.

"Alo-who?" Wavey further inquired.

"Alopecia, it's a condition that causes partial or complete hair loss from areas of the body where it normally grows," Patrick explained.

"Oh, that explains a lot. How long has it been like this?" Braidy asked.

"For a while now. But this past school year it's gotten really bad and all the students here at Tangletown think it's a joke. Especially the Frizz twins." Patrick finished his sentence, a little embarrassed. Braidy rolled her eyes.

"Ugh I can't stand those annoying boys. They think they can just try and bully students and get away with it," Braidy said annoyed. "If it makes you feel any better, we're not having a great time at Tangletown either. It is almost as if Wavey and I feel alone here. I guess people look and treat us differently because our hair isn't like theirs and that's not fair." Braidy confessed to Patrick.

"That is exactly how I feel. No one understands anything about me or my condition, but are just so quick to judge. I hate it here."

Braidy and Wavey moved around Patrick and gave him a group hug to comfort him.

"Hey Patrick," Wavey added as he pulled away from the embrace.

"Yeah, what's up?" Patrick asked.

"Mind if we call you Patch?"

Braidy laughed and added, "It is kind of a cute nickname, and it fits." The three of them laughed until Patrick agreed.

"Fine, Patch it is."

As they continued to talk on the bus, they attempted to get to know each other more. During their conversation, Wavey instantly had an idea. "Hey Patch, I know we are about to be at school and the students are always joking about your hair, but I have an extra Durag in my bag. I think you should have it." Wavey pulled out his silky green durag and gave it to Patch.

A "du-who?" Patch asked, mocking Wavey.

Wavey laughed and answered, "It's a durag. That's what I'm wearing now. Not only does it look cool, but it helps to keep my hair down so that I can have 360 waves," Wavey explained.

"Ohh, so that's how you got your hair to be like that?" Patch asked, admiring Wavey's style.

"Well there's more to it than just this, but this plays an important part. Stick around long enough and I can teach you the secrets." Wavey helped tie the durag on Patch's head and the students on the bus watched intrigued.

"Where can I get one?" A student called out.

"I got these from a beauty supply store in my hometown, NewComb City. I'm not too sure where in Tangletown you can get them", Wavey replied proudly.

"Well I think I want a black one," one student called out.

"Yeah, I want a purple one," another chimed in.

"I want a silver and red one." Different students continued to shout out.

"Yeah, it's lit!!" Patch said loudly. The students who barely heard Patch ever speak were shocked to hear his voice so loudly.

"He gets one little scarf on his head and now he can talk," Fade snickered.

"Someone sounds jealous," Braidy shot back as she laughed.

"Yeah, yeah, whatever." Fade shrugged as he and his brother looked at everyone interacting with Braidy and Wavey, with a look of envy on their faces.

CHAPTER SIX

As the bus pulled into Tangletown, more and more students noticed Braidy, Wavey, and Patch. That was the most attention they have ever received during their time at Tangletown! The three stepped off the bus to find Mr. Licer standing in front of the school, eyeing all the students carefully as he normally does.

"He better not say anything to me," Braidy said as they drew closer to him.

"Why would he?" asked Patch.

"Well, it's a long story." Braidy said, cutting off Wavey before he had a chance to speak.

"Oh, well in that case I hope he doesn't say anything to me either. You think we can get in trouble for this?" Patch asked, pointing to his new durag.

"We shouldn't, but who knows what can happen at Tangletown." Braidy answered, shrugging her shoulders.

The three walked past Mr. Licer hoping he wouldn't say anything to them. "Well good morning," he blurted out with a stern voice. "Glad to see you covered that mess up," he added.

Braidy stopped in her tracks. Before she could turn around, Wavey tapped her, "C'mon sis, don't pay him any mind. The only mess he needs to worry about is all that lice on his head." Patch and Braidy busted out laughing.

"You're right, he has bigger problems on his hands." Braidy joked back. The three of them laughed as they entered Ms. Frobe's classroom and took their seats.

"New look? I like it," Ms. Frobe says observing their new looks.

"Why thank you, I styled all of us myself," Braidy joked.

Ms. Frobe took attendance and when she called for the Frizz twins, everyone noticed that they were not present.

"Weren't they on the bus with us earlier?" Wavey asked.

"Hmm that's strange," Braidy said aloud, wondering where they were since they were not in class. Ms. Frobe began the lesson for the day. Meanwhile, the Frizz twins took a quick detour to Mr. Licer's office before going to class.

"They need to take those things off! It's distracting to us and I'm sure everyone in the class feels the same way. We can't seem to concentrate with them wearing that." Buzz claimed to Mr. Licer.

"Yeah, the bright colors and the way it looks on their head is getting too much attention from the other students and we need you to stop them," Fade added. But truthfully, the Frizz twins were just jealous of all the attention Braidy, Wavey, and Patch were receiving from their peers. Since they were on the bus, students were looking at them intrigued. And then the compliments and questions began to follow. "I love how this looks on you," one girl told Braidy. "Cool style," another student mentioned to Wavey. Even Patch was being noticed by peers he had never spoke to! "Love the look, "one of the students told him while passing him in the hallway.

All of this extra attention that they were receiving infuriated the Frizz twins and their anger and jealousy caused them to go to Mr. Licer. "Alright, I know exactly what I'm going to do. We can't have our students getting distracted by some stupid scarf or whatever they call those things," Mr. Licer explained to Buzz and Fade in his office.

"Perfect," said Buzz with an evil grin on his face. The Frizz twins happily walked out of the office smiling, knowing that this was going to harm Wavey, Braidy, and Patch in some way. "We gotta get them outta here," Buzz said as they walked the halls proudly. The Frizz twins entered the classroom and as they sat down, Mr. Licer made an announcement on the loudspeaker.

"Please pardon the interruption. Will Braidy Stylez, Wavey Stylez, and Patrick Growth please come to my office IMMEDIATELY!"

Ms. Frobe and the class displayed a look of confusion, while the Frizz twins busted out laughing. As the three of them walked out of the classroom, Fade whispered, "Good luck Braidy Bunch," which made the twins seem suspicious to everyone else.

"I know they have something to do with this," Braidy said as she walked while staring at the Frizz twins. As they made their way to the office, Patch started to get very nervous. "What's the matter," Braidy asked him.

"I just don't want to get in trouble, that's all," replied Patch.

"If anything, just blame Braidy," Wavey joked.

"This is serious," Braidy scoffed angrily. The three arrived at the front of the office and took a deep breath. Braidy was first to knock on the door.

"Come in," Mr. Licer said in a stern tone . The trio entered with three different facial expressions. Patch was scared, Wavey displayed a blank expression, and Braidy was visibly upset. They entered and found Mr. Licer with his arms folded, sitting down at his desk with an angry look on his face. Mr. Licer refrained from offering them a seat and immediately began to speak.

"The reason why you were called to my office is because of the extremely inappropriate behavior you guys have displayed here at Tangletown these past couple of weeks." He directed his attention at Braidy and Wavey. "I am also surprised to see you following in their footsteps, Mr. Growth," shifting his attention at Patch.

"What do you mean, what did we do wrong?" Braidy interjected.

Mr. Licer laughed, "What did you do wrong? Well first you come in with these ridiculous hairstyles that we've never seen before, and then you want to wear your little colorful scarves on your head." Mr. Licer sarcastically claimed.

"It's called a durag," Wavey jumped in.

"Well, IT'S UNACCEPTABLE!" Mr. Licer shot back with a stern voice.

"Well, you told us to cover up our hairstyles and that's exactly what we did," Braidy added.

"I know what I said, but this isn't your old school where you can wear whatever you want and get away with it. It's distracting to all the students here and many have complained to me already."

"I bet it's only distracting to the F rizz twins," Braidy stated matter-of-factly.

Patch gained the courage to defend themselves and added, "Everyone else thinks it's pretty cool," Patch muttered under his breath.

"I've had enough! Get rid of those things on your head and get rid of them for good!" Mr. Licer shouted.

"We could wear our hair however we feel comfortable. Back in NewComb, we felt at home. So, we should be able to do the same here!" Wavey argued.

"Well, why don't you just go back to NewComb then and do that," Mr. Licer added.

"THIS IS WHY I HATE IT HERE!" Braidy yelled, as she stormed out of the office.

Wavey and Patch quickly followed her. As they walked back to Ms. Frobe's classroom, they heard another announcement on the loudspeaker. "Please pardon this interruption, there will be no durags of any sort on school grounds! Also, all Tangletown students must follow ALL the rules in terms of hair/hairstyles. If you fail to comply, you will face serious consequences. No exceptions!"

CHAPTER SEVEN

Tangletown students began to talk amongst themselves as they watched Braidy, Wavey, and Patch walk the halls back to their classroom.

"What happened?" One student asked them.

"Mr. Licer doesn't know anything, the durag looks great," another complimented.

"Will you guys be coming back here?" Another student in the hall whispered.

As the trio arrived back at class, they walked straight to their seats and put their heads down in sadness. Meanwhile, Buzz and Fade watched and laughed from a distance. Ms. Frobe noticed what was taking place and started to piece things together. She waited a moment and suddenly composed a solution to the trio's problem.

"I need everyone in the class to please put their desks in a circle. Also, Buzz and Fade please come to the front of the classroom. I need you both to do something for me," she instructed.

"Why? What did we do?" The Frizz twins asked, confused as to why they had to face the stares of their entire class.

"I didn't say you two did anything and you're not in trouble. Please, just come to the front of the classroom," Ms. Frobe reassured them.

"Fine," the Frizz twins muttered.

The whole class formed a big circle where each student had a clear view of each other. Braidy, Wavey, and Patch put their desks in the circle, but quickly put their heads down after. When the Frizz twins reached the front of the classroom, Ms. Frobe handed them both a marker.

"What's this for," Fade asked.

Ms. Frobe smiled and provided the twins with clear instructions. "I want you two to write these words on the board, and then tell the class why you think I made you write them." Ms. Frobe handed Fade a piece of paper. He unfolded the paper and noticed three words written boldly: "BULLYING, RESPECT-EQUALITY".

The twins wrote the words onto the board and turned towards the class. "We finished," Frizz called out.

"Well answer the question, why do you think I wanted you two to write these words down?"

The twins stood in front of the classroom completely puzzled. Ms. Frobe sat down and waited for their response just like the rest of the class. Braidy, Wavey, and Patch still had their heads down and did not want to be bothered.

Suddenly, Fade had an answer. "Ohhh, Ms. Frobe I know why," he started. Patch lifted his head, curious to hear what Fade was going to say. "Well, you wanted us to write about bullying because that's what happened to us. We always show respect, and we treat everybody in Tangletown equally," Frizz answered confidently.

"Great answer, Buzz." Fade stated. The twins began to laugh, only to realize that the rest of the class including Ms. Frobe was not amused by their joke.

"This just isn't fair," Patch said with a low voice. However, it was loud enough for those around him to hear.

"What's that, Patrick?" Ms. Frobe asked. The class became dead silent and awaited Patch's answer.

Braidy nudged Patch and said under her breath, "Well aren't you going to answer?" Patch looked around the classroom and took a deep breath.

"I SAID THIS JUST ISN'T FAIR!" Patch yelled out.

Ms. Frobe's eyes widened, and the Frizz twins became startled, which caused them to drop the markers. The rest of the class looked at Patch in shock. They had never heard him speak, let alone yell.

"So, what isn't fair, Patrick?" Ms. Frobe asked.

"This school, this principal; everything. Ever since I got to this school, students have picked on me, some students don't want to talk to me, and some think they know me or know why I'm like this. But they really don't." The class grew more engaged, including the Frizz twins as Patch continued. "The same goes for Braidy. People want to treat her differently just because of how her hair is, but that's just life and no one understands that this is a hairstyle that makes her comfortable; that makes HER HAPPY! No one understands the reason why my hair is like this. Plus, Braidy and Wavey didn't even need to know in order for them to be my friends." The class grew silent for a moment.

"So, then why is it like that?" Fade asked.

"The truth is that I have a condition." Everyone's eyes widened even more, including Ms. Frobe.

"A condition?" A student asked.

"Yes, a condition called alopecia and that's why I have these bald spots on my head." Some of the students put their heads down in shame.

"So, will the spots ever grow back?" A student asked further.

"Yes, hopefully after I receive treatment." The Frizz twins left their spots at the board and joined the circle.

"Is it contagious? We don't wanna get it," Buzz asked.

Fade nudged him and whispered, "Shut up, Buzz." Patch rolled his eyes.

"No, it's not contagious and no one is gonna get it, you big baby." The class laughed.

"Hey, hey. Settle down," Ms. Frobe interjected, as she attempted to calm the class down. "Buzz or Fade, is there anything you'd like to share with the class?" Ms. Frobe asked.

"To be honest, Buzz and I only get these haircuts because our mom makes us."

The class laughed and the twins instantly felt embarrassed. Braidy and Wavey also laughed a little. Ms. Frobe walked to the front of the classroom and picked up one of the markers. She circled the words and drew a line on the circles connecting them. "Buzz, Fade, and to the rest of the class, the reason why these words are on the board is because I wanted to explain how important they are and how one relates to the other. Bullying someone causes harm to someone one way or another. What you say to others can hurt them and cause them to feel less of who they are. When you bully, it means that you don't have RESPECT for that person, their feelings, or their wishes. Having respect for one another is very important. Respect means that you accept somebody for who they are, even when they're different from you or you don't agree with them. But when you lack respect for someone, that means that you do not treat them equally and everyone in this class is equal. There isn't a student here who is better than anyone else. I want you all to know and understand this from this day forward, until you reach my age, and the years beyond that."

CHAPTER EIGHT

R ING, RING, RING!!!

The bell for recess sounded and the students rushed out of the classroom. As they headed towards the door, Ms. Frobe called after them, "Remember what I told you and don't forget it."

Braidy, Wavey, and Patch trailed behind the rest of the class while the Frizz twins remained at their desks. Ms. Frobe, not realizing that the Frizz twins were still in the classroom, began to clean off the chalkboard.

"WAIT, NOT YET!" Fade shouted.

Ms. Frobe was shocked as she turned around and noticed the two sitting down with their notebooks and pens out. "I didn't notice you two were still here. Is everything alright?" she asked.

"Yeah, Fade thought it would be a good idea for us to write the words down before we went to recess," Buzz answered in a dull tone. Ms. Frobe rewrote the words and moved out of the way so they could see.

"So, how did you feel about today's lesson?" She asked them once seated at her desk. The twins looked around and hesitated to answer. "Well, I don't know how you feel until we talk about it," Ms. Frobe added.

"I mean I thought it was alright," Fade answered.

"Okay, that's a good start. And what about you Buzz?" Buzz took a long pause.

"It was good, I *guess*," he answered sarcastically.

"Well that didn't seem like a very genuine answer," Ms. Frobe replied.

"I just feel like you did all this just because the stupid Stylez twins and Patrick got into a lil' trouble with Mr. Licer earlier," Buzz let out. Ms. Frobe paused for a minute before responding.

"A little trouble? Well Mr. Licer seemed very angry on the loud speaker and even banned durags throughout the entire school. That sounds like big trouble to me." Buzz and fade just sat there and listened. "You two wouldn't happen to know how they got in trouble, would you? Because it would be a shame if our own students would do something like that to their fellow classmates." Ms. Frobe continued, already suspecting the two. They remained silent for a few more minutes, feeling guilty of their recent behaviors.

" BUZZ DID IT !" Fade shouted.

"Nuh uh," Buzz mutters.

"YES! It was all your idea." The two began to bicker with each other until Ms. Frobe interjected.

"STOP IT!" she yelled. "Now, tell me why did you do it and I don't care who speaks. I just want the truth." Ms. Frobe added, sternly. The Frizz twins looked at each other, scared. "Well?" Ms. Frobe said while waiting with her hands on her hips.

"We went to Mr. Licer and told him that the durags were distracting us and everyone in the school so they shouldn't wear them. We knew that he didn't like their original hairstyle so it would just make them get in more trouble and they would just want to leave Tangletown for good."

Ms. Frobe stood in complete shock as she stared at the twins with her eyes wide. "Now why would you do all that? What did you gain from it?" She asked, awaiting a logical answer.

"We're supposed to be the only set of twins here, Buzz and Fade Frizz. That's it! We don't need the Stylez twins coming, trying to steal all of our shine." Buzz blurted out.

"Yeah, and it looks like they added that Patrick kid to their little group too.

Soon, it'll be the entire class, then the whole school," Fade jumped in.

"I don't think that's what they were trying to do. They just got here and now they are in all sorts of trouble because of you two bullying them, not showing them respect, and not treating them equal." Ms. Frobe replied, as she pointed to the words in their notebook. "If anyone should be in trouble, it should be you two," she continued, angrily.

Fade and Buzz put their heads down. Ms. Frobe began to put the desks back in their original form in order to get the class ready for the remainder of the day. Ms. Frobe eventually reached Buzz and Fade's desk and they did not want to move. "Excuse me gentlemen, you can go to recess now."

"We just want to say we're really sorry, Ms. Frobe," the twins let out through crocodile tears.

"I'm not the one you should be apologizing to, Braidy, Wavey, and Patrick are."

"Will they accept it?" Buzz asked.

"Well, that's up to them and how they feel." The two began to wipe their faces.

"You're right," Fade said as he wiped his nose.

"Try thinking of a way to make things better. Make it up to them in a special way. It would be much better than just a simple 'I'm sorry'." Ms. Frobe advised the boys.

The Frizz twins made their way to recess, thinking of ways to make their situation better. "Maybe we can just tell

Mr. Licer it's okay now and we're not distracted anymore." Buzz suggested.

"Ehhhhhh," Fade started. "I think it's too late for that. The damage has been done already," he replied.

"How about we write them a card? Who doesn't love a good card." Buzz also suggested.

Fade laughed, "A card? We're in junior high school. That's baby stuff. Besides, what is a card going to do?" Fade asked.

"Well, do you have any ideas?" Buzz shot back.

"How about we get our own durags and wear it with them?"

"So, you're saying to get the very same thing that we told on them for?

Wouldn't we just look like hypocrites?" Buzz asked, confused.

"I mean, it's either that or get braids, and I don't think we can do that," Fade said sarcastically. Buzz stood still with a puzzled look on his face. "Well? What do you think?" Fade pressed.

"It's not a bad idea, but it's going to have to be more than just us. Like who else would join us? The rest of the class?" Buzz suggested.

"We gotta come harder than that. We need to get the whole Tangletown Jr. High!" Fade exclaimed.

"The whole school?" Buzz asked, still puzzled.

"Yes, the whole school! We can even ask Ms. Frobe to wear one, too. That's the only way we can make a real difference, if everyone is involved." Fade finished.

"Hmm, I like the idea. Maybe you are the smarter brother after all," Buzz joked.

"Maybe? More like definitely!" Fade returned. "Now let's go back and tell Ms. Frobe the idea."

The two ran back to Ms. Frobe's classroom. While doing so, Mr. Licer noticed them in the hallway. "And where are you two gentlemen speeding off to?" He asked, standing in front of the boys with his arms crossed.

"Oh, umm, we just forgot something in the class. That's all." Buzz nervously managed to let out.

Mr. Licer stood there, scratched his head and told them, "Alright, just be careful and stop running before you hurt yourselves.

"GOT IT," Buzz and Fade yelled in unison, power walking to the classroom. "Ms. Frobe! Ms. Frobe!" The Frizz twins yelled.

"It's recess time, what are you guys still doing here?" she asked.

"We wanted to tell you about the idea we came up with to help Braidy, Wavey, and Patrick." Fade answered.

"Well, that was fast. Let's hear what you got." Ms. Frobe sat down to listen to their ideas.

"Sooo, Buzz and I were thinking, and we wanted to make the whole school wear durags on Monday. You know, to show support to them." Ms. Frobe began to smile.

"That's a great idea!" Ms. Frobe let out, excitedly. "I'll even get one to support also," she added.

"Perfect! Fade and I will start spreading the word to all the students and tell them to get one so that they can wear it to school on Monday. It's going to be the biggest thing to ever happen at Tangletown Jr. High!"

CHAPTER NINE

The Frizz twins spent the rest of their Friday afternoon informing all the students at Tangletown about their secret plan. "Come to school with a durag this Monday, spread the word, but don't tell the Stylez twins or Patrick Growth." They told the students as they passed them in the halls. Braidy, Wavey, and Patch were unaware of what was happening and went about their day oblivious of the plan that the Frizz twins were putting together. As they walked through the hallways, students shouted words of encouragement to keep their spirits high.

"It's going to be alright, we got you," a few of the students who knew of the plan assured them.

"I wonder what they're talking about," Patch asked, confused as to what was taking place.

"Who knows, maybe they're just trying to be funny," Wavey shrugged off.

As the day came to an end and the students made their way to the school bus, as usual they encountered Ms. Frobe outside watching them being dismissed. Braidy noticed and immediately got upset.

"Ughhh I wish we didn't even have to see his face" she says. As they walk out of the school, Mr. Licer spotted the trio heading to the bus and shouted,

"Remember what we spoke about, and I'll see you Monday!" He said with an evil grin on his face. The trio heard him but completely ignored him because they didn't want to turn around.

"I can feel all that lice from here," Patrick joked. They eventually made their way onto the bus after a long week of school.

Meanwhile the Frizz twins were hard at work getting their plan across to the rest of the students. "Durags Monday! Durags Monday!" was one of the text messages that was sent to many of the students at the school. Before boarding the school bus, they informed the other teachers, school officials, custodians, cafeteria staff, the other bus drivers, and even the school nurse to wear a durag. Everyone appeared curious and asked them what their reason was. "It's to support our fellow students for a good cause." Fade explained.

"Do you think they'll actually wear them?" Buzz asked after a while.

"I sure hope so. The more the merrier and we gotta make a statement!" Fade exclaimed. The Frizz twins boarded the bus, excited about their upcoming plan. As they walked past Braidy, Wavey, and Patch who sat next to each other, Fade gave a nod and a smile to Braidy. *Don't try and be all nice now*, she thought in her head as she caught wind of his friendly gesture. The bus took off and made its way towards everyone's home.

"I'm surprised it's so quiet on here." Patch whispered to Braidy and Wavey.

"Maybe Buzz and Fade had a long day and are too tired to be their normal selves." Braidy whispered back.

Wavey laughed, "Whatever it is, I'm just glad we don't have to deal with it."

"Right!" Braidy and Patch answered in unison.

The bus made its first stop and to Patrick's home. Followed by the Frizz twins, and lastly, Braidy and Wavey. After they hopped off the bus, Wavey quickly dove into his bag to put on his durag. "Mr. Licer can't say anything here," he snickered.

"You got that right," replied Braidy as she followed in her brother's footsteps. "Hey Wavey."

"What's up?" he answered.

"Even though we aren't allowed to wear durags anymore, I just want to say thanks for trying to find a way to make things better and support me. It means a lot." Braidy let out, as she gave her brother a tight hug.

"That's what I'm here for, you know I always got your back." He answered with a smile. As he hugged his sister, he felt her braids and then asked her about them. "So, what are you gonna do about your hair now?" She paused for a moment before answering.

"I don't know, to be honest I don't want to take out the braids."

Wavey wrapped his arm around her and replied, "Well no matter what you do with it, it will still look good."

"Thanks, Wavey," Braidy smiled confidently at her brother.

When they reached home, Braidy and Wavey found their parents sitting down on the couch watching tv. They joined them and began talking about the school day

"So what'd the lice man say?" Ms. Stylez asks jokingly referring to Mr. Licer.

"He thought the durags were cool," Wavey said followed by an awkward laugh.

"Did he really? Ms. Stylez asked suspicious of Wavey.

"Yeah he even said he was gonna buy one for himself." Wavey joked.

Mr. and Ms. Stylez sensed something was off based off their son's tone.

"Wavey just tell them the truth." Braidy says after taking a deep sigh.

"Well?" Mr. Stylez asks while waiting for someone to speak.

"Truth is, we got in trouble today for wearing the durag." Wavey said.

"I knew we should have been the ones to handle this! We're going there first thing Monday morning to have a word with him "Mr. Stylez tells Ms. Stylez."

"Definitely! So what happened? What did he say ? Ms. Stylez asked Braidy and Wavey.

He called us into the office and said the durags were "distracting" and how students were complaining about it and made a whole announcement on the loud speaker saying that they are banned from the school"

"All that for a durag? Ms. Stylez asked.

"Yes," Braidy replied.

To be honest , all this is causing too many problems. I don't even want to have this hairstyle if it's going to make it such a big thing.

"Braidy what ? No you love that Style, that's your signature look don't say that. Just let mom and dad handle it," Wavey says to his sister.

No Wavey, I'm just tired of everything this is causing. It got us detention, made mom and dad upset, got Patrick in trouble. Is it even worth it? Let's say if mom and dad do handle it, then Mr. Licer is just going to have his eye on me, and I don't want to deal with all that. Its best I just change the style and save everyone the trouble. I'm over it. Braidy says in defeat.

As the weekend came to a close, Braidy began taking out her braids and combing out her hair While doing so, many thoughts began to run through her head. NewComb, Mr. Licer, the Frizz twins, and even Patch. She became annoyed, angry, sad, but most of all hurt that she can't wear her favorite hairstyle to school anymore. To make matters worse, she can't even wear her desired alternative to cover it up. Before the night was over and it was time for bed, Braidy looked at her calendar to count how many days were left before going back to NewComb for vacation.

"I guess I can wait a few more weeks till I'm home again," she assured herself. She crawled under the covers, turned off the light and went to sleep hoping to have a better week of school.

CHAPTER TEN

Braidy and Wavey woke up for school and followed their normal routine. Wavey saw his sister and was surprised to see her hair straightened and not with her hair not in braids.

"Smile, you look fine," he said as he tried to cheer up his sister.

"Fine, I guess I just miss wearing my Braids, that's all." Braidy replied.

The Stylez twins made their way to the bus stop and as the bus rolled in, they stood there puzzled to see all of the students on the bus wearing durags. "Wait, what?" Braidy asked rhetorically. They boarded the bus and even noticed the bus driver wearing one.

"This gotta be some type of joke or something," Wavey said to Braidy.

The two sat down looking around at all the students on the bus in their durags. The bus picks up Patrick, who also didn't receive the durag message.

"Guess none of us got the memo," Wavey mentioned to Braidy as he noticed Patch from a distance. Patch got onto the bus and had the same surprised look as Braidy and Wavey.

"Soooo, is something weird going on or is it just me?" Patch asked the twins.

"Bro, we thought the same thing," Wavey replied. "This is crazy."

The bus made its last stop before arriving at school, and the Frizz twins hopped on both wearing their own durags.

"Time out. So, is it like wear a durag to school day because now this is crazy." Wavey blurted out. The Frizz twins walked past them on the bus and Fade gave Braidy that same smirk and smile he gave her the last time they saw each other.

The bus reached Tangletown Jr. High and as the trio looked out the window, they were completely shocked to see every one of the students wearing all different types of durags as they entered the building. "Uhhhhh, I think we're at the wrong school." Patch stated while scratching his head. From the window of the bus Braidy, Wavey, and Patch noticed Mr. Licer livid, as he watched all the students in confusion and anger.

"Well, someone looks angry," Braidy joked. The three exited the bus and were immediately approached by a furious Mr. Licer.

"I know you three have something to do with this!" he shouted at them.

"Hey, you don't see us wearing durags. We did exactly what you told us to do," Braidy quickly answered.

"Yeah, we got nothing to do with this." Wavey jumped in.

"I'm going to get to the bottom of this and whoever is responsible is going to be very, very badly punished" Mr. Licer exclaimed.

"Well, we hope you find that person cause it sure ain't us," Braidy uttered as they left Mr. Licer standing there.

The three walked away and laughed on their way to class as they noticed all the different durags that the students were wearing. When they entered Ms. Frobe's classroom, they noticed her wearing one too.

"MS. FROBE?!" Braidy shouted.

She laughed, "What's the matter, Braidy?" She asked.

"Well, can someone tell us what's going on?" "Have a seat and we will explain everything to..."

"ATTENTION! ATTENTION!" Ms. Frobe was suddenly interrupted by the loudspeaker.

"I need all faculty, staff and students to report to the gymnasium immediately for an emergency assembly!" Mr. Licer shouted angrily.

"Well, all I know is we better not get into any more trouble," Braidy muttered.

Ms. Frobe led the class to the school gymnasium to find everyone wearing a durag. All the students, teachers, and everyone who worked in the school could be seen with one on.

"Great, I wish we could've worn ours," Wavey mentioned to Patch and Braidy.

As they waited for Mr. Licer to speak, more students entered the gym the same way. This only made him more upset than he already was.

"He's so mad, the lice on him is scared," Braidy joked, and the students nearby laughed.

"May I have your attention please!" Mr. Licer shouted on the microphone. The noise in the gym lowered as everyone shifted their attention to him. "Last week, I made the announcement specifically banning durags, and today you all are wearing them. I need whoever is responsible for this to please step forward!" Silence ran through the room, and you can hear students whispering in fear.

"It wasn't my idea."

"I didn't do it."

"I thought it was for a good cause."

These were just a few things that the students whispered amongst themselves.

"If I have to investigate, the punishment for those responsible will be much worse." All the students looked around, but no one was willing to say anything.

"IT WAS US!" The Frizz twins finally screamed in unison.

"I BEG YOUR PARDON!" Mr. Licer yelled in shock.

"YES, IT WAS US!" Fade admits.

"So, you mean to tell me that you two, Buzz and Fade Frizz put this whole mess together?" He asked them in disbelief.

"We did because we realized how you were treating Braidy and it wasn't fair.

Ms. Frobe laughed as Mr. Licer replies, "It wasn't fair? I find it funny that it would be you two after the both of you came to my office to complain about how those durag things were so distracting." All of the students gasped.

"Snitch!"

"Tattle tale," the students began whispering under their breath.

"I knew it!" Braidy said, shaking her head. "Of course they would try and get us in trouble," she added.

"Yes, we did tell you that but then we also realized that what we did was wrong. You see Mr. Licer, you were just like us. You acted like a bully, that didn't show Wavey, Patrick, and especially Braidy any respect and as a result, they weren't treated equally. We got everyone in Tangletown to wear the durags because Buzz and I felt as though she should be able to wear her hair however she wants. So, until she can wear her hair in Braids we are all keeping the Durags on!" Fade stated boldly.

Ms. Frobe smiled and looked at the Frizz twins with a-thumbs up. Mr. Licer became furious. He felt as though he was betrayed by the Frizz twins and the whole school was against him. Meanwhile, Braidy, Wavey, and Patch were still surprised that all this was taking place.

"Maybe the Frizz twins aren't that bad," Braidy whispered to Wavey and Patch.

"Well, I didn't see all this coming," Patch admits.

"I want everyone involved to remove those stupid things from your heads NOW!" Mr. Licer shouted out. The gym remained silent, and everyone kept their durags in place.

"Guess we can't all get in trouble," Patch softly let out.

"My class, line up and make your way towards the door." Ms. Frobe shouted to her class that was scattered in the gymnasium.

"And where do you think you're going?" Mr. Licer asked.

"I have a class to teach now," Ms. Frobe replied sternly.

As the class left the gym, the other teachers followed and instructed their classes to do the same.

"WHERE ARE YOU ALL GOING!?
"Mr. Licer shouted.

"To teach the students of Tangletown how to treat others equally and with respect!" A teacher shouted back from across the gym as she led her students back to class. As more and more classes left, Mr. Licer realized there was nothing he can do. He stood in the gym until he was the only one left to think to himself of the events that just took place.

As the day came to an end, Ms. Frobe sat at her desk and felt her durag, which had started to get sweaty. "Whew, these things could make you hot," she said to break the silence.

The Frizz twins laughed, "Tell me about it. Fade and I are hot, but we're not taking it off until we're home." Buzz stated as he put his books away. Braidy overheard their conversation and started talking to the Frizz twins.

"I just want to thank you guys for sticking up for me, my brother and Patrick. It was nice of you to do that for us." Wavey and Patrick joined in and expressed how they felt as well.

"Yeah, thanks a lot guys. Mr. Licer is something else." Wavey added.

"It's the least we could have done. Besides, we were pretty mean to you guys before and we regret it." Buzz apologized.

"And, sorry to you too, Patrick." Fade added.

"It's alright. Hey, just call me Patch from now on."

The Frizz twins looked at Patrick and smiled, "Hey, that fits." They all laughed.

Meanwhile Mr. Licer went to his office and thought of what he should do. Pacing in his office angrily he felt a sense of powerlessness. He took his time to think of different punishments he can give and realized that he cannot punish the whole school. He was put in a position that he had little room to do anything. After taking time to think he finally makes a decision.

"ATTENTION! ATTENTION!"

Mr. Licer can be heard on the loudspeaker. "Everyone settle down, Mr. Licer is speaking," Ms. Frobe hushed her students.

"After much thought and consideration, I have decided to lift the rule on braided hair here at Tangletown Jr. Highschool. The students at Tangletown should be able to wear their hair in the way that makes them most comfortable in the classroom so it can be easier for them to learn and excel here at this great school. Also, I will allow durags for those students who wish to wear them. Thank you and have a good day."

The class erupted in a loud cheer as Braidy smiled ear to ear and started to do a happy dance. Shortly after, the class joined in and started dancing as well.

"YES!" she shouted out. She ran and gave her brother and Patch a big hug. Right after, Ms. Frobe and then she even hugged the Frizz twins. "Thank you so much, guys. I miss my old school at NewComb City, but this is going to make me feel a lot more comfortable and happier here."

Meanwhile, Wavey, Patch, and the Frizz twins were still dancing in the middle of the classroom. "Come finish what you started," said Patch.

Braidy thought for a second, "Only if Ms. Frobe dances with us."

"You know I'm too old for those kind of things." Ms. Frobe said, jokingly.

"C'mon, no you're not," Braidy said as she pulled Ms. Frobe into the circle.

The class danced for the rest of the day until the bell rang for dismissal. Ms. Frobe asked the class, "How did this end up turning into a party anyway?"

The class yelled in unison, "BLAMEEEEE BRAIDYYYYYY!!!"

About the Author

Ron Philippe was born in the Bronx, New York in the mid-90s. His love for writing began in high school where he wrote a number of pieces for his school's newspaper. Ron attended and graduated from the State University of New York college at old Westbury. He got a job as a substitute teacher working with students from all ages. Although Ron has always had an interest in writing, he didn't pick it up right away. Working as an educator required him to write and sparked his interest in writing again where book ideas began flowing in his mind. Hence, his debut book is in the works.

Currently, Ron Philippe works as a special education teacher teaching kids with moderate to severe disabilities. He uses his position to inspire his students to constantly think outside the box so that they can be successful.

Made in the USA
Middletown, DE
19 July 2021